OTHER YEARLING BOOKS YOU WILL ENJOY:

YEARLING BOOKS are designed especially to entertain and enlighten young people. Patricia Reilly Giff, consultant to this series, received her bachelor's degree from Marymount College and a master's degree in history from St. John's University. She holds a Professional Diploma in Reading and a Doctorate of Humane Letters from Hofstra University. She was a teacher and reading consultant for many years, and is the author of numerous books for young readers.

A Big Box
of Memories

Judy Delton

Illustrated by Alan Tiegreen

A YEARLING BOOK

Published by
Dell Yearling
an imprint of
Random House Children's Books
a division of Random House, Inc.
1540 Broadway
New York, New York 10036

Visit us on the Web! www.randomhouse.com/kids
Educators and librarians, for a variety of teaching tools, visit us at www.randomhouse.com/teachers

ISBN: 0-440-41528-4

Printed in the United States of America

March 2000

10 9 8 7 6 5 4 3 2 1

CWO

Contents

For Dorfee Tucker, with thanks for the
popcorn balls, cigars, and fireside chats,
and mostly for our long-going,
on-going friendliness

CHAPTER 1

Old Lady Molly

"This is an important year," said Mrs. Peters to the Pee Wee Scouts. "Can any of you tell me why?"

The Pee Wees all frowned as if they were thinking hard. Molly Duff had found that if she looked as if she were thinking very hard and did not put her hand up, she didn't get called on. Especially at school in classes she was not good at, like math. She always had her hand up if it was a spelling lesson or reading, no matter how hard the words were.

But now no one had their hand up to be called on. No one seemed to know why it was an important year.

"Easter?" said Tim Noon. "Or Memorial Day?"

"Every year has Easter and Memorial Day," scoffed Rachel Meyers. "That doesn't make it a special year. Just an ordinary one."

"Was it the coldest year in Minnesota?" asked Mary Beth Kelly, who was Molly's best friend. "My mom said it was the snowiest winter she could remember."

Mrs. Peters frowned. "It may have been," she said. "But that's not why this year is important."

"Maybe it'll be the warmest year," said

Tracy Barnes to Molly. "Last summer was so hot we went swimming every day."

"It has nothing to do with the temperature," said their leader mysteriously. "Think harder."

The Pee Wees did.

"I know," said Tim Noon. "It's the year my uncle got married!"

"Pooh," said Sonny Stone. "My uncle got married too. That's no big deal. People get married every day."

"And divorced," said Lisa Ronning. "That's not news."

The Pee Wees thought some more. Why didn't their leader just tell them?

"I know why the year's important," said Rachel. "I really do."

Before Rachel could tell everyone, Patty Baker waved her hand. She was Kenny's twin sister. "It's election time,"

she said. "We elect a new president this fall."

Everyone agreed that was important. Even Mrs. Peters.

"But this news is important to everyone in the world," she said.

Now Rachel waved her hand.

"It's the first year of this century, Mrs. Peters," she said importantly.

"That's right, Rachel! The twentieth century is over. And this year begins a whole new hundred years! The twenty-first century. Is everyone used to writing the year yet?"

The Pee Wees laughed.

"I keep writing 1900," said Tracy Barnes.

"It's a big change," said their leader.

Rachel sighed. "It's the biggest change in a thousand years," she said. "Now it's the year 2000. The new millennium."

"Good for you, Rachel!" said Mrs. Peters. "One hundred years ago, we went from 1899 to 1900. Now it's one hundred years later, and 1999 has changed to 2000."

"My great-great-grandma was born in 1900," said Molly. "My mom did our family history. We have a picture of her in a long dress. There were no cars, only horses then."

"Good for you, Molly," said Mrs. Peters. "Lots of changes have taken place in one hundred years. In the year 2100, pictures of our clothes will look as strange to people alive then as the ones of 1900 do to us."

Molly tried to picture what people would look like in another hundred years. Would they have long dresses again, and horses? Or would they have antennas coming out of their heads, and little airplanes in their garages instead of cars? She shivered. She wouldn't even be alive then! Unless she lived for more than a hundred years! She didn't know anyone who had lived that long!

If she was 107 in the year 2100, she would be old and wrinkled and walk with a cane. Or not walk at all! Her hair would be gray like her grandma's. She might even be in a nursing home! Molly's imagination was wild, her mother said, and she was right. Molly got so lost in being an old, old lady that her arms and legs felt achy. Suddenly Mary Beth said cheerfully, "We'll all be dead by 2100!"

"I don't want to be dead!" cried Sonny Stone, who was a baby about a lot of things. He still had training wheels on his bike, even though he was seven.

"That's a long time away," said Mrs. Peters. "And right now we want to think about being alive this year, at the turn of the century. We want to think about what the Pee Wee Scouts, especially Troop 23, can do to celebrate and mark the occasion. Does anyone have any ideas?''

CHAPTER 2

The Pee Wees in a Tube

"I think we should have a great big party," said Roger White, "with a lot of good food and noisemakers and stuff. A party that lasts all night!"

Some of the other Pee Wees cheered and clapped and chanted "Party! Party! Party!"

Mrs. Peters frowned. "A party is a good idea," she said. "But we can have a party anytime. I was thinking of doing

something more important. Longer lasting. So that Pee Wee Scouts in the year 2100 will know just what we were like back here in 2000."

"We could take a group picture," said Patty. "That would be the best way."

"That's a good thought!" said Mrs. Peters.

"A picture would get all ripped and torn and wet in a hundred years," said Kenny. "It wouldn't last."

"Unless," said their leader mysteriously, "we put it in a very, very safe place."

"Do you mean hide it, Mrs. Peters?" asked Mary Beth.

"If we hide it, they might never find it," said Kevin Moe. "And anyway, how do we know they would find it in a hundred years instead of ten years, or two hundred years?"

"We wouldn't exactly have to hide it," said their leader. "We could put it in a very safe place and let people know where it is and when to look at it."

Rachel had a big grin on her face. "I know what you mean," she said. "You're talking about a time capsule! We put lots of stuff inside a big tube and put the tube in cement somewhere and write on it 'Open in 2100.' "

"That's right, Rachel," said Mrs. Peters. "A time capsule is a perfect Pee Wee Scout project. The city is building a new city hall this year, and it will have a cornerstone. On the outside the cornerstone will have the date, and on the inside there will be room for historical records. That will be just the place to put a Pee Wee Scout time capsule for future generations to see."

Now the Pee Wees were getting excited.

"We'll go down in history," said Kevin.

"People will know how we lived, even after we're dead!" said Jody George, who was in a wheelchair. Molly liked Jody. He was smart and kind and a lot of fun. He let the Pee Wees ride in his chair once in a while. Molly liked Kevin too. He was very ambitious. He might even become president someday. He had told her so.

"I'm glad you're all excited about doing this," said Mrs. Peters. "Let's talk about what the children of 2100 would like to know about us. What could each of us leave behind for them to see how we lived?"

The Pee Wees couldn't stop talking. They were full of ideas.

"I'm going to leave my bike!" said Sonny.

"With the training wheels on it?" roared Roger.

"You can't leave something that large," said Jody. "The stuff has to fit into the time capsule, doesn't it, Mrs. Peters?"

Their leader nodded. "Jody is right," she said.

Jody is always right, thought Molly.

"The time capsule is about this big," said Mrs. Peters, showing them with her hands. "About two feet long, two feet high, and two feet deep. And we aren't the only ones putting something into it. The city officials and the schools will make contributions too.

"The Pee Wees will have a little metal box with our names on it," Mrs. Peters went on. "It will say 'Troop 23,' and each of us will put one item inside. We'll have to think very hard about what to choose, because each of us can put only one small thing. It should say something special about each of us. I'll start our collection with the Pee Wee pledge and song. And maybe, if there is room, one of each badge that we have earned."

The Pee Wees were thinking hard. This isn't as easy as it sounds, Molly thought. Things like her favorite sweater or her Pee Wee scarf were probably too big to include.

"If I can't put my bike in, I'm going to put in a snowball so they can see how much snow we have in Minnesota," said Sonny.

"You can't," said Roger. "Snow melts. There'd just be a puddle of water in the bottom of the box."

"The box would rust," said Lisa.

"The water would evaporate," said

Jody. "Then there would be nothing left from you."

How smart Jody was! He was so scientific. No wonder I like him, Molly thought. Maybe if she married Jody someday they could both be scientists and discover cures for diseases like head colds. Molly hated to cough and sneeze in the winter.

"Besides," said Mary Beth, "they wouldn't want to see snow. They could see snow themselves if they looked out their windows. Minnesota isn't going to change that much in one hundred years, is it, Mrs. Peters?"

"Probably not," she laughed. "It will probably still snow in Minnesota in 2100. We'll really have to put on our thinking caps for this one. We want whatever you choose to be about *you*. We want it to be small and lasting and well chosen. You

need to think this over for a while. We'll have a week or so to decide. When the mayor gives us our box, we'll put the things into it carefully, all labeled neatly. When we finish, we'll get our Time Capsule badges!"

"Yay!" shouted the Pee Wees. It would be fun to fill the box, and it would be more fun to get a badge for it!

Rat's knees, thought Molly. Badges are what Pee Wee Scouts are all about!

CHAPTER 3

Barrettes and Baseball Cards

Molly felt nervous about making such an important choice. This badge wasn't like a baby-sitting badge or a dog-walking badge. This badge was for what her grandma called posterity! Molly wasn't sure she could think of a perfect item all by herself. But it seemed babyish to ask her family for help. Earning a new badge was a challenge. Molly liked to think she was up to it.

On their way home, the other Pee Wees

didn't seem to take the job as seriously as Molly.

"Hey, I'm going to put in my math paper I got a C on," said Tim Noon.

"A C!" shouted Rachel. "You should only put an A paper in!"

"Tim never got an A in his life!" said Lisa.

"I'm going to put in some cereal," said Kenny. "Frostibites, my favorite."

"They'll disintegrate," said Kevin. "Food dries up. I'm going to put in a baseball card. They may not play baseball in 2100. It will be valuable."

Molly couldn't believe how fast her friends had made up their minds. Mrs. Peters had said to take some time. She'd said it was very important. They were reaching into the future. It wasn't just a badge for making cookies.

Roger was chasing Sonny down the

street. He'd forgotten all about his important decision. He was trying to put a night crawler down Sonny's shirt.

Mary Beth was talking to Patty about a movie she had watched on TV.

Why was Molly the only one who worried so much about these badges? Why did she worry about *everything* more than the other Pee Wees?

How could Kenny decide on cereal so fast? It wasn't a good choice.

And Kevin's baseball card. That wasn't bad, but wouldn't something else be even better? Molly wanted the very, very best thing of all. The thing that would tell the most about her in 2100. A baseball card said something about Kevin, but not much. It didn't say how smart he was and how he would be mayor or even president someday.

"Aren't you guys worried about what to choose?" asked Molly, stamping her foot on the sidewalk. "Don't you want to pick the best thing you can think of?"

Mary Beth and Patty stopped laughing about the movie and looked at her.

"We've got a couple of weeks to think about it," said Mary Beth.

"It's an easy badge," said Tracy. "The easiest one we ever got. Remember when we had to ski? That was hard."

"And when we went to the ranch and had to square-dance," said Mary Beth. "That was something to worry about. Not as dumb as what to put in a tube. I'll just put my hair barrette in. That's small, and it's pretty."

She took the barrette out of her hair and said, "See? I'm all ready."

Molly couldn't believe her ears. Her

friends were making a joke of the time capsule!

When Molly got home, she went to her room to think. She got out her pencil and paper, sat at her desk, and made a list. She felt better with a pencil in her hand. Lists made her feel good. She liked to cross off things she'd done, throw the list away, and start a new one. Her mother said lists were a habit with her. Like brushing her teeth or making her bed.

Molly picked up her pencil. But what in the world should she write? Well, she'd write the title. "Things to put in the time capsule to remember Molly Duff by in 2100." Then she put the pencil behind her ear and looked out the window. When the phone rang, she jumped.

"Hey, this is Roger," said the voice on the phone. "I was wondering what you're going to put in the capsule."

What a surprise! Roger *did* care about this badge!

"I haven't decided yet," said Molly. "I'm thinking about it."

"Well, when you decide," said Roger, "will you get two of them?"

"Two of what?" asked Molly.

"Two of what you're going to put in."

"Why?" asked Molly.

"So you can give me one to put in," said Roger.

Molly was disgusted. She should have known Roger's interest was selfish.

"You need something that's about *you*," said Molly. "Not me!"

"I don't care who it's about," said Roger. "I just need something, or I won't get my badge."

"Rat's knees!" said Molly. "Forget it. Do your own work."

Roger was taking time away from her

work and making her angry while he was at it. She said good-bye and hung up.

Molly thought and thought till she got tired. "I'll take a little nap," she said, stretching out on her bed with a yawn. Badges were hard work.

And then she fell asleep.

By the time her dad called her for supper, she had dreamed that she'd finally
found just the right thing to put in the
capsule. It was a magic ring. When she
rubbed it, it showed pictures of every-

thing that had happened in her life. It would show the Pee Wees of 2100 just how she lived. It was perfect!

But just as she was about to pop it into the capsule, Roger ran up and grabbed it away from her. When she chased him out into the street, he dropped it. It fell down the storm sewer and was gone forever!

CHAPTER 4

The Perfect Thing for the Capsule

"It was just perfect!" cried Molly. "I'll never find another one anywhere!"

"What was perfect?" said her father. "You must mean me! And you're right, you'll never find another one—but you won't need one! One perfect dad is enough!"

Molly laughed. "It was a dream," she said. "It was a dream about Roger."

"Well, speaking of someone who isn't perfect . . . ," her dad laughed.

"You can say that again," said Molly.

"Speaking of someone who isn't perfect . . . ," her father repeated, tickling Molly under her chin.

Molly's dad was a lot of fun. And he *was* close to perfect, thought Molly.

At supper Molly mentioned the new badge.

"I'd put my bowling trophy in, I think," said her mom thoughtfully.

"It's too big," said Molly. Anyway, Molly didn't bowl. It wouldn't do her any good.

"I'd put in my new fish scaler," said her dad. "That's small enough, and people would know how we scaled our sunfish back in 2000."

Molly didn't fish. Her mom and dad weren't much help.

"Molly should put in one of her famous lists," her dad went on, taking another piece of pizza. "The kids of the future could see how organized she was."

Molly thought about that suggestion as she cleared the table. After dessert she went to her room and decided that a list might be a good idea. But a list of what? What would say the most about her life?

A list of chores, a list of what she did all day, a list of books she'd read?

All of a sudden, she had it! Her diary! Molly's diary was like a story of what she did and how she lived. It would be perfect for the kids of 2100! She was so excited, she couldn't wait to begin! But when she looked at her diary, she realized it was too big for the capsule. Rat's knees! Nothing was ever easy. Then she had a great idea. She could copy her diary into a very small notebook. She would have to do teeny-tiny writing to make everything fit. The children in 2100 would probably be able to read small writing because they would have very good eyesight by then. Doctors would probably have discovered pills or shots for people to take instead of wearing glasses or contacts.

Molly found a small notebook in her desk drawer. It had an old list of things she wanted for Christmas in it. But Christmas was over and now she really wanted a teeny-tiny diary.

She tore out the used pages and threw them away. Then she sat down and wrote "Diary of Molly Duff, Pee Wee Scout, 2000. By Molly Duff," she added.

She very carefully copied some entries in very small writing. She remembered fun things she had done. "Went swimming in the park." And "Roger pushed Rachel off her bike. He's mean." She

found she could get a whole week of the diary on one little page if she took her time and wrote carefully.

So many good things had happened, Molly thought. She wrote until her hand got tired, and then she got ready for bed. Her mom came up to brush her hair and tuck her in.

"No TV tonight?" her mom asked.

"I was too busy," Molly answered. "Working on my project."

"Good," said her mom, giving her a good-night kiss.

In the morning before school, Molly wrote some more in the notebook. She had fun remembering Jody's birthday party. The Pee Wees in 2100 would have fun reading about it, she thought.

After school she raced home and kept writing. She wished she could write with her left hand, because her right hand ached. The next day she wrote more, and the next day more than that. Rat's knees, she thought, this is a lot of work. She hoped Mrs. Peters would appreciate it. And the Pee Wees of 2100.

By the time the next Pee Wee Scout meeting came, she had only a few more weeks of her diary to copy. She was almost finished!

Some of the Pee Wees had things ready for the capsule.

Tim gave Mrs. Peters a rusty fishhook. "I caught my first fish with this," he said proudly.

Kevin had his rare baseball card. "Think how valuable that will be in one hundred years!" he said. "It's worth ten dollars even today!"

Mary Beth handed in her blue barrette.

Sonny had a bottle cap. "Bottles won't have caps then," he said. "This will be valuable too."

"I doubt it," said Mary Beth. "Who wants a dirty old bottle cap?"

Then the Pee Wees told their good deeds and ate their cupcakes. When they were done eating, Roger walked up to Molly and whispered, "Have you got it? Have you got something for me to put in the capsule?"

"You have to get your own!" said Molly. "I'm putting my diary in."

"Oh," said Roger eagerly. "Make a copy for me too."

Molly stamped her foot. "It's a lot of work to copy my diary," she said. "It takes a long time!"

"I can wait," said Roger.

"You don't want *my* diary," she went on, "with *my* name on it!"

"I'll change the name," said Roger. "Easy. I'll just cross your name out and write mine on the cover."

"What a dumb idea," said Mary Beth when she heard. "He's so lazy! Who'd want someone else's diary? It would be like a lie."

"Roger would do anything to keep from having to work," said Rachel.

"Well, he's not getting my diary," said Molly. "Rat's knees, it's a lot of work."

"But it's a good idea," said Rachel. "I think it's the very best idea of all. It's what kids would really like to read in 2100."

Mary Beth agreed. Molly was glad to hear her friends say this. She was glad she had thought of it.

"I'll have my capsule piece ready next Tuesday," she told Mrs. Peters when the meeting was over.

"That's the last day," their leader warned her.

Mrs. Peters didn't have to warn her. Molly was reliable. What could possibly keep her from having her diary ready on time?

CHAPTER 5

Emergency!

Molly decided not to take any chances. When she got home, she went to her room and finished copying her diary. Finally it was done! Her badge was a sure thing!

She closed the little notebook and tried to think of the safest place to put it until next Tuesday. She didn't want any harm to come to it before then. And she didn't want anyone to find it. Molly remembered seeing a TV show that said to hide

valuables in an unusual place, somewhere a burglar wouldn't think to look.

A burglar would look in a desk first,
she thought. Notebooks and diaries go in
desks. Then she remembered that on the
TV show, the person put her valuable
jewels in a soup can and put it in the refrigerator. What a good idea! Molly had
learned some valuable things from TV!
She could take the soup can from her
dad's lunch, wash it out, and hide her
notebook in it!

Molly dashed downstairs. No one was
around. Perfect! She took the tomato
soup can out of the recycling bin and
washed and dried it. She tucked the notebook in it and put it on the top shelf of
the refrigerator, near the back. Now she
could relax, like the other Pee Wees. Her
project was done, and it was a good one.
The very best. She wished she could be

around in 2100 to see the expressions on the faces of the children who would open her diary and read it. They would say, "Oh, Molly sounds like such a great person! I wish she were still around so we could meet her!"

Molly could almost see those children. Instead of books they probably would carry little computers. Smaller than her dad's laptop. Maybe they would never have seen a real notebook before till they saw Molly's! Molly would be someone historical, like the children in the Little House books. Maybe somebody would even publish her diary as a book! Children would stand in line in bookstores when it came out! They would ask for it in libraries. Teachers in 2100 would read it to their classes. Molly would be famous! Maybe they would even make a movie of it. Very often, she knew, books became movies. If Molly was in a movie, everyone would remember her. Like Cinderella or Tiny Tim.

This was more than a badge—this was a historical landmark!

Suddenly the front door slammed and Molly jumped. For a minute she had forgotten where she was and what year it was! Her imagination again!

"I'm home!" called Mrs. Duff.

Molly helped her mom get supper. Then she called Mary Beth to tell her the news.

"I'm glad you finished it," said Mary Beth.

"It was worth all the work," said Molly. "It could be a book, you know, or even a movie."

"Really?" said her friend. "Isn't it too short for that?"

"It's long," said Molly. "It looks short

because the writing is so small. Anyway, they get those screenwriter people to make it bigger. They put in lots of action and stuff. They'll get some kid like Roger to play Roger. Some kid from 2100."

"I don't know . . . ," said Mary Beth. "No one could play Roger but Roger."

When the weekend came, Molly was glad she didn't have any badge worries. She rode her bike and went to Tracy's house to play Monopoly. Her project was safe and sound, waiting for Tuesday.

On Sunday she got her library books together to take back on Monday. She decided to get her notebook out of the refrigerator and put it in the bag she always took to Pee Wee Scouts. Molly liked to be ready ahead of time.

She ran into the kitchen. The sun was shining through the window and sparkling on the clean floor. It was quiet.

The clock ticked and the refrigerator hummed.

Molly opened the refrigerator and reached in the back for the tomato can.

But there was no tomato can!

She decided not to panic. She looked on every shelf. Then she took everything out of the refrigerator so she could see better. She pulled open the vegetable crisper and the meat keeper. And even the freezer. No tomato can!

Where was it? Had a burglar found it, even though it was hidden so well? Had the burglar seen the same program on TV about hiding things? Had Roger come and taken the can from the refrigerator? But he didn't know it was there. And he couldn't have gotten into her house without a key!

Where was that tomato can?

Molly's stomach began to ache the way

it did when she got a bad mark on her report card. Or when she had made up a little fib and knew she shouldn't have.

Molly's mother and dad came home from taking a walk.

"Have you seen my tomato soup can that was in the refrigerator?" Molly asked.

"Soup can?" said her father.

"I think I did see a soup can in the refrigerator," said her mother. "I wondered how it got there. Your dad ate all the tomato soup."

Her mother opened the refrigerator and looked. She moved things around.

"It's gone now," she said.

"Why do you want a soup can?" asked her dad.

Tears rolled down Molly's face. "It was my project," she said. "My diary to put in the time capsule was in that can."

"Why was it in the refrigerator?" asked her mother.

"So it would be safe," sobbed Molly. "From burglars."

Her dad looked as if he might make a bad joke, but he changed his mind.

"I saw it on TV," said Molly. "But they were wrong. It wasn't safe. It's gone."

"I don't know how it could have disappeared," said Mr. Duff. "We're the only ones using our refrigerator. Unless Skippy took it." Skippy was Molly's dog.

Molly could hardly smile even at the funny thought of Skippy opening the refrigerator door and taking the soup can out with his paw.

Suddenly Mrs. Duff snapped her fingers.

"I think I know what happened," she said.

CHAPTER 6

Second Best

"Mrs. Noon!" she said. "She cleaned the kitchen for me when I was at work! I'll call her."

Mrs. Noon was Tim's mother. She cleaned houses for a living. Molly liked her. But how could she have thrown out Molly's important Scout project?

When Mrs. Duff came back into the kitchen, she was frowning.

"Mrs. Noon remembered it," she said.

"She cleaned out the refrigerator. She thought the can was empty and she threw it out. The truck picked it up on Friday. I'm sorry, Molly."

The trash. The truck had taken her precious diary for the space capsule to the recycling center. Maybe she could go to the center! But the center was big. Huge. Things were put into machines and scrunched up. Her notebook was absolutely, positively gone.

"Can you get another one?" asked her dad.

Molly shook her head. "It takes a long time to write so much in little tiny writing," she said. "And it has to be little to fit into the time capsule."

She showed her dad her regular diary. "It's too big," she said.

"We'll help you copy it again," said Mr. Duff.

But Molly did not want her parents reading her personal diary! Diaries were private! Especially from parents. They couldn't copy it without reading it!

"It's all right," said Molly. "I'll get something else."

But what? Molly had to find something else to put into the time capsule, and she had to find it fast. What in the world would it be?

Molly ran to the phone and called Mary Beth. She needed help. This was no time to be proud. She needed other minds to work on this.

"I'll call Rachel and the others," said Mary Beth. "We can meet at my house in an hour and talk about what to do."

Mary Beth and some of the other Pee Wees were on the Kellys' front porch when Molly got there. Mrs. Kelly brought out a plate of fresh cookies.

"I'm so sorry to hear the bad news," she said to Molly.

Rat's knees, everyone knew about Molly's problem. People felt sorry for her! Even parents.

But it was great to have friends. Friends cared about her. Friends would help her!

"It's pretty late to start all over again," said Rachel, biting into a chocolate chip cookie. "I'm glad I turned mine in early."

This did not feel like help to Molly. It made her feel worse.

"We'll think of something," said Lisa. "There are lots of things that would be good."

"None as good as that diary," said Mary Beth. "That was really cool."

"What's your favorite food?" asked Jody.

"Food doesn't last a hundred years," said Molly.

"Some does," said Jody. "Like wine and cheese. They age and get better."

"My grandpa had a bottle of wine that was fifty years old," said Mary Beth.

"I'm sorry to be so fussy," said Molly, "but I don't like wine or cheese. It has to be something I like."

The Pee Wees kept thinking. And they kept eating cookies. Then they were thirsty, and Mary Beth's sister brought out glasses of milk. This was turning into a party. A what-in-the-world-will-Molly-do-now party. But Molly did not feel in a party mood.

"Why don't you just put in an old hair ribbon or something?" asked Lisa.

"Yeah, or a pencil you used, or a note-book," said Tracy.

The mention of a notebook reminded

Molly of her diary, and she felt like cry-
ing. She didn't want to hear the word
notebook for a long time.

"You always have to be different," said
Roger, who had been riding by on his
bike and had smelled the cookies.

Molly hated those words. They were
what her mom often said to her!

"It's okay to be different," said Jody.
"It's just that it's a lot of work."

Molly felt warm toward Jody. He knew
how she felt! He knew it was okay to
want something that was not ordinary.

"Molly is creative," said Rachel. "Like
artists and writers. It takes more to please
them."

"It's her imagination," said Kevin.

Rat's knees, her friends were talking
about her as if she weren't there! As if she
were some weird person who thought
she was better than anyone else. She

didn't. She just didn't like to be second best.

She looked at Roger, who never worried about things. And Sonny, who couldn't care less what he put in the capsule. He and Tim were busy taking the chocolate chips out of their cookies, throwing them in the air, and catching them in their mouths.

"All right," said Jody. "I think the first thing to do is make a list of Molly's interests. We have to think of what kind of thing she'd like to be remembered by."

Mary Beth got some paper and a pencil. Jody wrote the number 1 on it.

"Do you like sports?" asked Kevin.

Molly shook her head. She didn't mind playing softball in the empty lot in summer, but it was definitely not her favorite thing.

"If you liked football, you could have had my Vikings cap to put in," he added.

Molly did not want to be remembered in 2100 for a Vikings cap. But it was nice of Kevin to offer.

"Thanks anyway," she said.

"How about a hunk of your hair?" said Kenny. "My mom has my first curl from when I was little in my baby book."

Molly did not think her hair was that important. What did her hair say about her? Especially if it wasn't on her head!

"That would be small," said Mary Beth helpfully. "And it would last."

"What are your interests?" asked Jody, still waiting to write something after the number 1.

"You like movies," said Lisa.

"And pets," said Tracy.

Jody wrote those down.

"I mostly like to read," said Molly. "And write. That's why I liked the diary. It was my favorite thing to do, and it told all about me."

Jody wrote that down. "So reading and writing should be number one," he said.

"Well, the diary is gone and that's that," said Rachel. "I have an idea. Let's have a treasure hunt! A treasure hunt for Molly's best thing! Whoever finds the best thing gets a prize!"

"Who will give the prize?" asked Tracy.

"I will," said Rachel. "I have two copies of the same video game. I'll give one of them away."

The Pee Wees liked video games. They all looked interested now.

"We could divide up and look all over town," said Lisa.

"I think the first place we should look

58

is Molly's house," said Rachel. "That's where there would be something personal. Something all Molly's."

The Pee Wees were trying to be helpful. But Molly knew her own house. What could they find there that she hadn't?

CHAPTER 7

The Hunt

"I guess a treasure hunt would be a good thing to try," said Molly.

"What we should do, then," said Jody, "is hunt for an hour and then bring the stuff back here. Molly can choose what she likes the best."

Jody looked at his watch. "Come back here at four o'clock. The one who finds the treasure gets the prize!"

Jody made it sound so easy! Weren't

friends great? That was what Scouts were for, to help others. And Molly needed help.

"Will your mom care if we dig around your house?" asked Patty.

"I don't think so," said Molly.

Molly, Patty, Mary Beth, and Rachel went to Molly's house. The other Scouts followed. Molly told her parents what they were doing.

"Good luck," said Mr. Duff. "I'll keep my eyes open too."

The Scouts went their separate ways. Even Molly looked again.

At four o'clock the Pee Wees went back to Mary Beth's house. Mary Beth's sister gave them some lemonade. Hunting had made them thirsty.

"What did everybody find?" Mary Beth asked.

"Look at this!" shouted Roger. "This is the treasure that gets the prize!"

He held up a rusty nail.

"This is an attic," he said.

The Pee Wees roared. "An attic?" shrieked Rachel. "I'll bet you mean an *antique*."

Roger turned red. He needs a dictionary, thought Molly. But he probably wouldn't read it.

"It's old," said Roger. "And valuable."

"Pooh," scoffed Lisa. "It's not old, it's just a rusty nail that you can get blood poisoning from if you step on it."

"I'm not going to step on it," said Roger. "I'm going to put it in the time capsule."

"Did anyone else find anything?" Mary Beth asked.

"How about Skippy's bone?" asked

Patty, holding it up with two fingers. It was slimy and wet.

"It would smell," said Molly. "Besides, it isn't mine, it's Skippy's."

Rat's knees, Molly sounded fussy. Even to herself.

"I found this little pinkie ring," said Rachel. "It's too small for Molly to wear now anyway. It's a baby ring."

Patty shook her head. "It doesn't say anything about Molly," she said. "It could be from any baby."

"What have the rest of you found?" asked Mary Beth.

Jody had found a pair of sneakers. Kevin had found an old doll. Kenny had found a plate of leftover cake Molly had baked. But nothing was right.

Finally Molly said, "I think I might have found the right thing in a box in the basement." She held up an old book. "I used this when I learned to read. It's a teeny-tiny little dictionary. My dad gave it to me. I liked words even then." She would put the dictionary in the time capsule! It would stand for Molly!

"It's perfect!" said Mary Beth. "Can we see it?"

"I didn't want to lose it, so I left it at home," Molly said. "But you'll see it tomorrow."

"Rat's knees!" said Rachel. "I wanted to find the best thing!"

The rest of the Pee Wees looked unhappy that they had not found the treasure.

"You'll get the prize yourself," said Patty. "For finding your own treasure!"

"Someone else can have the prize," said Molly. "If we hadn't had the treasure hunt, I wouldn't have found the dictionary!"

Molly was relieved. When she got home, she'd put her name and address and the year in the little book. She would get it ready to take to Mrs. Peters's house the next day. Ready for the time capsule. It was no diary, but it was definitely second best.

Molly wished she had a prize to give all the Pee Wees for trying so hard to help her. But she couldn't waste time on that now. She had to get home and get the dictionary ready. It was almost Tuesday. Almost the deadline for the time capsule. Molly had never been a last-minute person. But now she was just under the wire.

She ran all the way home. She opened the door and ran in to pick up the book from the hall table where she had left it.

But it wasn't there! The table was empty. It was shiny and clean, and there was nothing on it. Nothing at all.

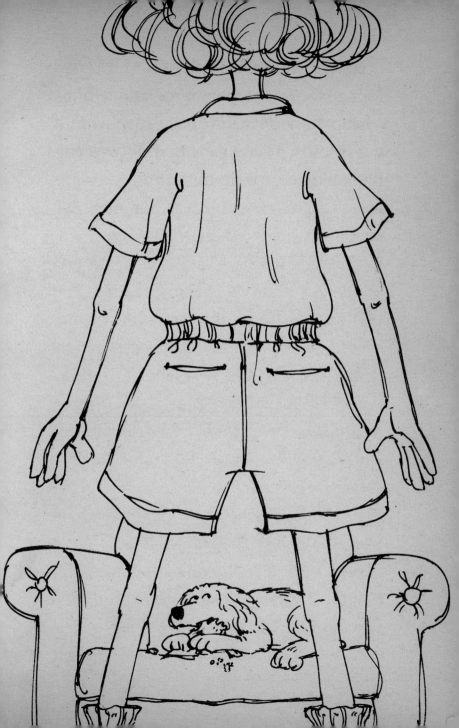

Skippy was curled up in Mr. Duff's chair. He was chewing on something. When Molly got closer, she saw what it was. Molly's dictionary! Skippy was eating her time-capsule treasure!

CHAPTER 8

Night Visitors

Why was Molly the only one to have lost two treasures? Why couldn't Skippy have eaten a different book? A scary book, or a boring book that nobody wanted? Why did Skippy have to eat a book at all? He had dog food in his dish that would have tasted much better.

"It was the leather cover," said Mrs. Duff when she heard the news. "Dogs like leather. They make dog bones out of leather. Skippy thought it was a dog bone."

Molly was sure Skippy was smarter than that. A dictionary didn't look like a bone. But it probably smelled like one.

Molly wanted to scold Skippy. But he had such an innocent look on his face. It wasn't his fault the dictionary smelled like a bone.

"What am I going to do?" she cried. "There's no time to find something else now!"

"You're going to have to settle for something not quite as good as what you wanted," said Mr. Duff.

Never, thought Molly. She would not settle. She would go to the meeting and hope Mrs. Peters would have a good idea. And hope that she could have an extra day to find the perfect thing. The perfect thing was out there somewhere, but Molly had no idea what it was or where it was.

Molly hardly slept that night. When she did, she dreamed that Skippy followed her to the Pee Wee Scout meeting and ate up the time capsule with all the Pee Wees' things in it! Skippy became a time capsule himself!

When she woke up, she was glad to find out it was only a dream.

At the Pee Wee meeting, Molly told her sad story.

"Rat's knees," said Mary Beth. "You better just take my barrette like I told you to."

"I wish there was some way you could put your diary in after all," said Jody thoughtfully. "But it's just too big."

"I think the time capsule should be big-

71

ger," said Tim. "I want to put in my Snoopy alarm clock. It doesn't work anymore."

Mrs. Peters shook her head.

"It can't be bigger," she said. "The box has to fit into the space in the cornerstone."

"Why did they make the space so small?" asked Sonny. "That's dumb."

"You aren't supposed to put your whole house in it!" said Lisa. "Just a memento."

Tim looked as if he was thinking very hard.

Jody looked as if a lightbulb had gone on over his head. He looked as if he had a brilliant idea. But he didn't say anything.

"Well, Molly," said Mrs. Peters, "I can only give you until tomorrow afternoon to come up with something. We have to get our capsule to the courthouse in time for the ceremony."

When Molly got home, she threw herself into a chair on the porch. Suddenly she saw Tim walking by. He was walking fast. And he was carrying a shovel.

Molly went to her room. When she came down an hour later, Tim walked by again. This time his shovel had dirt on it. So did his jeans and T-shirt. He looked tired.

Then, after supper, he returned with the same shovel.

"Where are you going?" Molly called to him.

"It's a surprise," he said. "Tell you later."

What could Tim possibly be digging that would be a surprise for *her*?

Night crawlers? Rocks? More treasure?

Nothing could help her now. She

would just have to grit her teeth and take the barrette Mary Beth had offered her. The barrette would have to be her gift to the children of 2100. That was all there was to it.

When Molly was playing with Skippy in the basement, she thought she heard the doorbell ring. Who would come to visit this late? When she looked out the basement window, she saw a car drive away. It looked like Jody's van. The one his wheelchair fit into. But why would Jody come to her house? And why would he come at night?

This was a mystery.

When she went upstairs, she said, "Who was at the door?"

"What door?" her dad said innocently. Molly hated it when people answered a question with another question.

"The front door!" said Molly.

"Maybe a salesman?" said her father.

Molly's mother frowned. "It was Jody," she said. "He stopped by to say hello."

This was even more mysterious! Why would Jody come at night to say hello to her parents and not her? And why would her father pretend he hadn't come? What was going on?

The news was on TV, and her father was watching.

"Tomorrow will be cloudy with perhaps a few showers," said the announcer.

When the weather report said there would be a few showers, there usually was a thunderstorm with lightning. Just like in winter, when they would say snow flurries, and a blizzard would cover Minnesota with three-foot drifts.

"And now in the local news," one of

the announcers was saying, "we have the town's youngest criminal! A seven-year-old boy was apprehended this evening for damaging city property by digging up the courthouse lawn! He was taken to the county jail and released into the custody of his mother. Well, we hope that after this the young man will do all his digging in his own backyard!" The three announcers behind the desk all smiled and made little jokes about a child-size jail.

Molly's parents stared at the TV. "Could we know that boy?" asked her mother.

"No," said her dad. "Molly's friends wouldn't dig holes on other people's property!"

Molly couldn't believe her ears. Could the boy be Tim Noon? She had seen him with a shovel. What had Tim done? No Pee Wee Scout had ever been arrested before!

And why had Jody paid her parents a nighttime visit?

CHAPTER 9

Jody to the Rescue

The phone rang early in the morning. It was Mrs. Peters.

"We're having an emergency meeting this afternoon," she said.

"Molly will be there," said Mr. Duff.

"I wonder what the emergency meeting is about," said Mrs. Duff.

Probably it has something to do with Tim, Molly thought.

When Molly saw Mary Beth on the way to Mrs. Peters's house, Mary Beth called, "Did you hear about the boy who dug holes? I'll bet he gets sent away to a school for boys who get into trouble!"

When they met Tracy, she said, "Someone's in real trouble! I think his mom has to pay a thousand dollars for the hole he dug."

Molly couldn't hold it in any longer. She had to tell her friends what she knew. "I think the boy in all that trouble is Tim."

Her friends gasped. They could hardly believe it. "I'll bet this meeting is to say good-bye to Tim," said Patty. "I'll bet he goes to that island where they put dangerous criminals so they can't escape."

Molly was so worried, she didn't want to go to the meeting.

But when they got to Mrs. Peters's house, Tim was eating a Popsicle and did not look as if he was in trouble. He looked just the way he did before he was a criminal, Molly thought.

Mrs. Peters tapped on the table with her pencil. The Pee Wees were quiet.

"She's probably going to announce the good-bye party for Tim," whispered Mary Beth to Molly.

Rat's knees, thought Molly. She should have brought a present for Tim. A book to read in jail. But Tim didn't read much. Well, she could have baked a cake with a little saw in it so he could cut through the bars of his cell and escape. You would think Mrs. Peters would have baked a cake. But there was no good-bye cake on the table. No cake at all. And there were no good-bye gifts wrapped up in fancy paper either. If this was a party for Tim, there wasn't much spirit. Not even any balloons.

"I called you all here," said Mrs. Peters, "to be sure everyone has their item in for the capsule. The millennium committee needs our box a bit earlier than they had said."

The Pee Wees stared at their leader. That was all? That was why the meeting had been called?

Roger turned in his rusty nail with his name tied to it on a tag. Some of the other Pee Wees had changed their minds about their items and put different things in their place.

"Now the only one we are waiting for," said Mrs. Peters, "is Molly."

Molly had nothing.

Jody waved his hand. "Here's Molly's," he said. And he gave something tiny to their leader.

The tiny thing looked like a book. Could it be the dictionary, come back by some magic?

"When Tim said he wished the time capsule were bigger, I thought maybe a better idea was to make the items smaller," said Jody. "I remembered how important it was to Molly to put her diary in, but it was too big. And then I remembered the copy machine at my dad's office. It makes things smaller! It makes them as small as you want! So I asked my dad and we went over to Molly's and borrowed the diary and shrank it."

Molly was so surprised, she didn't know what to say.

"I didn't read it," said Jody quickly. "Not even one word. My dad took it back to her house right away."

Rat's knees! No wonder she wanted to marry Jody, Molly thought. He was one friend in a million. A friend who had saved her badge. A friend who had good ideas. Molly decided she loved Jody. She felt like giving him a big hug, even a kiss—but that wouldn't be a good thing to do at a Pee Wee Scout meeting.

Everyone clapped and cheered.

Roger whistled and shouted. "Let me have a look at that diary," he said, trying to grab it. "I just want to see how small it is," he said.

But Molly knew he really wanted to read it. She couldn't risk that. And she couldn't risk anything happening to it this time. She wanted her diary in that capsule as soon as could be!

"Yay for Jody!" called Kevin. "Why didn't I think of that? My mom has a copy machine too."

"Well, the important thing is that the problem is solved," said Mrs. Peters. "Jody was thoughtful and generous and saved the day. Now we all have something memorable in the time capsule, and we can all get our badges for this project."

As the Pee Wees ate the treats Mrs. Stone brought down to them, Molly looked at the tiny diary. It had no hard cover or lock, but none was needed. The important thing was that all the words were there! It was better than the one she had copied over in tiny letters! It was an exact picture of her real diary!

Everyone looked at it and told Jody how smart he'd been to think of it.

"Hey," said Roger. "Can you make me smaller if I sit on that machine? Or could you make me bigger, like a giant?"

Rachel groaned. "The only thing worse than Roger would be another Roger," she said. "A bigger one."

"Maybe Jody could shrink him till he was real little, and we could step on him!" said Patty.

Mrs. Peters frowned when Patty said that, and the Pee Wees stopped making jokes. But Molly secretly thought it would be fun to step on a teeny-tiny Roger. After all, Roger stepped on the Pee Wees when he had the chance.

Molly thanked Jody over and over again. She knew he hadn't read her diary, because he was so honest. And she was glad, because she had written things in there she didn't want him to see. She didn't want him to know she was going to marry him. It was too soon. They were too young.

CHAPTER 10

Badges and Prizes

"I guess this isn't going to be a party for Tim after all," Lisa whispered to Molly. "But I know he's going to be locked up," Molly whispered back.

"They have to have a trial first," said Lisa. "My uncle is a lawyer, and that's the way it works."

Rat's knees, Molly thought. They had to save Tim. The Pee Wees couldn't sit by and watch a police car take him off to be locked up. Molly wondered how much time she had to solve this problem.

She sighed. It seemed as if it was just one problem after another. The time capsule problem had just been solved, and she'd hardly had time to enjoy it. She had to work fast now to solve the next worry—how to save Tim.

She hoped she wouldn't have to go to court and sit in that box the way they did on TV. She'd have to swear to tell the truth, so help her God.

Well, that would be easy enough. She could truthfully tell the judge and the jury that Tim was a good Scout. How he'd taken home a cat that had no food and fed it. How he'd learned to spell some words even though they were hard. She'd tell them how he had never been in any trouble in his whole life. Well, as far as she knew. Molly hadn't known him as a baby, but what was the worst thing a baby could do? Throw toys or bite someone. She didn't think Tim had bitten anyone. She was almost positive.

After the treat some Scouts told about the good deeds they had done. Then Mrs. Peters clapped her hands.

Molly jumped. She had been thinking so hard of what she would say about Tim in the courthouse, she'd forgotten the meeting. She wanted to write her ideas down so she wouldn't forget them.

But their leader had something else to say.

"I'm sure you all heard the news last night," said Mrs. Peters. "And lots of rumors get started when something is on TV. Sometimes things that are not a big deal seem bigger when they're on the news."

"You mean like making mountains out of molehills, Mrs. Peters," said Rachel. "That's what my grandmother always says."

"That's exactly right," said Mrs. Peters. "Now, you all probably know by now that someone was apprehended by the police for digging a hole next to the courthouse and ruining a flower bed on public property. Well, Tim Noon was the boy on the news. However, no serious damage was done, and Tim now knows he should ask an adult before digging anywhere again."

"I don't have to dig anywhere now," said Tim. "I was trying to make more room for a bigger space capsule. I knew Molly wanted to put her diary in, and it would fit if I could dig a bigger hole. And I could get my Snoopy alarm clock in too. But now I don't need to. The diary fits

now. And my mom took my clock to be fixed so I can use it again."

Rat's knees! Tim had been digging a bigger hole for *her*! What a kind thing to do! Molly felt tears coming to her eyes. Whenever she was happy she cried. It was so embarrassing.

"That was a very generous motive," said Mrs. Peters. "But even though you were being helpful, Tim, you can't break rules and deface property."

"My mom is paying for the flowers," said Tim. "And I filled in the hole already. The police made me."

"Well, that's a happy end to a bad situation," said their leader. "And now we can move on."

So Tim wasn't going to jail or boys' school! His mother wasn't paying a thousand dollars! Molly had been worried sick again, all for nothing! When would she be able to get a grip on her wild imagination? How could she stop her mind from spinning make-believe tales? Rat's knees, it wasn't an easy habit to break!

"Mrs. Peters, I have something else to say," said Rachel. "I think Jody should get the prize for finding something for Molly to put in the capsule."

Then Rachel explained about the treasure hunt, and how no one had found anything suitable. But Jody definitely had come up with the right thing.

"That's a great idea!" said Molly.

"I'll give my extra video game to Jody," said Rachel.

"That's really nice," said Jody. "But I think Tim deserves the prize for trying so hard to make room for Molly's real diary."

Tim looked happy when Jody said that.

And of course Jody was right. Tim didn't have a video game. Jody probably had lots and lots of them. And Tim had been very generous. Risking his life to help Molly! No one could do more than that!

"That's a very good idea," said their leader. "If it's all right with Rachel, that's what we'll do."

Rachel nodded. Tim smiled. All the other Pee Wees cheered again.

"And now," said Mrs. Peters, with a deep sigh, "I think we'll wind up this emergency meeting by giving out the badges."

As their leader called out names, each Scout came forward to get the brand-new badge. It was a red badge with a little white time capsule embroidered on it. Underneath the capsule it said "2000."

Molly pinned hers to her blouse. At home her mom would sew it on her Pee

Wee scarf with all the others. It was fun earning the badges, and it was fun collecting them!

"Let's end the meeting and then go to the time capsule ceremony," said Mrs. Peters.

The Pee Wees made a big circle and joined hands and sang their Pee Wee song.

Molly held Jody's hand on one side and Tim's on the other. She sang more loudly than anyone else. So loudly that Sonny put his hands over his ears. But that didn't stop her.

Molly was happy.

She had a new badge. And the best friends in the world.

Rat's knees, Molly was glad she was a Pee Wee Scout!

Pee Wee Scout Song

(to the tune of
"Old MacDonald Had a Farm")

Scouts are helpers, Scouts have fun,
Pee Wee, Pee Wee Scouts!
We sing and play when work is done,
Pee Wee, Pee Wee Scouts!

With a good deed here,
And an errand there,
Here a hand, there a hand,
Everywhere a good hand.

Scouts are helpers, Scouts have fun,
Pee Wee, Pee Wee Scouts!

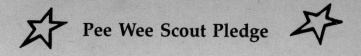

Pee Wee Scout Pledge

We love our country
And our home,
Our school and neighbors too.

As Pee Wee Scouts
We pledge our best
In everything we do.